UNDER THE MOON

Written by Vivian French

Illustrated by Chris Fisher

WALKER BOOKS
AND SUBSIDIARIES

LONDON • BOSTON • SYDNEY

For Davie,
with love

First published 1993 by Walker Books Ltd
87 Vauxhall Walk, London SE11 5HJ

This edition published 1998

2 4 6 8 10 9 7 5 3

Text © 1993 Vivian French
Illustrations © 1993 Chris Fisher

This book has been typeset in Plantin.

Printed in England by Clays Ltd, St Ives plc

British Library Cataloguing in Publication Data
A catalogue record for this book is
available from the British Library.

ISBN 0-7445-6382-8

Books are to be returned on or before
the last date below.

... the sky; a little boy who was tricked by a wily mother wolf; a sweet apple child and a sour elder bogle. Read about them all in this magical book of three stories.

Vivian French became a broadcast poet on *Children's Hour* at the tender age of six. Some years later, she worked in children's theatre, both as an actor and writer, and is now an author and storyteller. She has written many children's books, including *Zenobia and Mouse*, *Mary Poggs and the Sunshine* and two more collections of original fairytales, *The Thistle Princess and Other Stories* and *The Boy Who Walked on Water* (also illustrated by Chris Fisher). She is also the author of *A Song for Little Toad* (shortlisted for the 1995 Smarties Book Prize), *Lazy Jack*, *Princess Primrose* and several other picture books, as well as the Read and Wonder non-fiction titles *Caterpillar Caterpillar* (shortlisted for the 1993 Kurt Maschler Award), *The Apple Trees* and *Spider Watching*. She has four daughters and lives in Bristol.

Chris Fisher is the illustrator of the picture book *Princess Primrose*, the young fiction title *Pappy Mashy* (by Kathy Henderson) and a number of other children's stories.

CONTENTS

*Dust dust dust, polish polish polish, shine shine shine —
all day long she was busy.*

UNDER THE MOON

Once upon a time there was a little old woman and a little old man who lived together in a little old house. They would have been very happy but for one thing, the little old woman just could not sit still. Never ever did she sit down and share a cup of cocoa with the little old man. Dust dust dust, polish polish polish, shine shine shine – all day long she was busy.

The little old man began to sigh, and to grow lonely. While their ten tall children were growing up in their neat little house he didn't have time to notice how the little old woman never stopped working. Now, however, he liked to sit by the fire and dream, and he thought it would be a friendly thing if the little old woman sat beside him.

"You could knit a little knitting," said the little old man, "or sew a little seam?"

But the little old woman said, "No no no! I must dust and sweep and clean."

The little old man sighed a long sad sigh and went and put the kettle on. He sat down beside the fire with Nibbler the dog and Plum the cat, and Nibbler curled up at his feet and Plum curled up on his lap, but still the little old man felt lonely.

The little old woman went on sweeping the yard with her broom, even though the stars were beginning to twinkle in the sky.

One day there was a knocking on the door.

"Who's there?" asked the little old woman, running to open the door with her duster in one hand and her mop in the other.

"It's me," said young Sally from the cottage down the road. "My mum says you'm the bestest cleaner in all the village, and we've just got two new babies as like as two peas, and all the children running here and there with smuts on their noses and dirt on their toeses, and our mum was a wondering...?"

The little old woman didn't wait another moment. She picked up her broom as she ran through the door, and she fairly flew down the road to Sally's cottage. All day she polished and swept and scrubbed and by the time the stars were twinkling, the cottage down the road was as shiny as a new pin; as fresh as a daisy; as polished as a one minute chestnut fallen from the tree.

★ ★ ★

"Well well well," said the little old man as she hurried through the door. "There's a good day's work you've done. Would you like a little cocoa?"

The little old woman actually sat down.

Thank you kindly, my dear," she said. "Just a sip or two – and then I must polish our own little house." And she sat quietly beside the little old man for five minutes.

"This is fine and dandy," said the little old man, smiling. Nibbler laid his head on the little old woman's feet, and Plum purred happily.

"Just as it should be of a gentle summer evening," said the little old man.

"No no no!" said the little old woman. She drank the last drop of her cocoa and jumped to her feet. "It was very nice, but I must hurry hurry hurry." And she seized the duster and hurried off to the dresser full

*Nibbler laid his head on the little old woman's feet,
and Plum purred happily.*

of china to polish and shine. The little old man sighed, but it was a medium sized sigh.

"Five minutes is five minutes more than nothing," he said. Nibbler nodded his head.

The next day brought another knocking on the door.

"Who's there?" said the little old woman, running to the door with her dustpan in one hand and a broom in the other.

"It is I," said the parson from the church across the hill. "I have heard that you are the most wonderful cleaner in the county, and my church is full of mice and moths and mildew."

The little old woman jumped to her feet. She picked up her soap and a bucket as she ran through the door, and she hurried and scurried to the church across the hill. She swept and she dusted and she rubbed, and by the end the church was glowing as if a hundred candles had been lit inside.

"Well well well," said the little old man as she walked through the door. "There's another good day's work done. Could you fancy a cup of cocoa?"

"Thank you kindly," said the little old woman, and she sat down on the bench by the fire with a flop. "Just a small cup, and then I must scrub our own back yard." But she sat quietly with the little old man and with Nibbler the dog and Plum the cat for ten long minutes. Then, up she hopped and away she went with the broom in the yard.

The little old man sighed a very little sigh.

"What do you think, Nibbler? Isn't ten minutes ten whole minutes more than nothing?"

Nibbler nodded, and Plum purred.

The next day no one came to the house. The little old woman cleaned and rubbed and scrubbed her little house inside and out, and when the stars began to twinkle in the bluebell sky she was still swishing her soapsuds in the tub. Then there came a knock at the door – such a timid, quiet little knock you could hardly hear it. The little old woman hurried to see who it was, her hands wet and dripping.

"Who's there?" she asked.

Standing on the doorstep was a strange grey shadow of a man. His hair was long and silver, and his clothes were all a tremble about him.

"I hear," he whispered in a voice as soft as a bird's breath, "that you are the very best cleaner in all the ups and downs of the Earth?"

The little old woman nodded briskly. She

*Standing on the doorstep was a strange
grey shadow of a man.*

shook the water from her hands, and the drops flew through the air.

"How can I help you?" she asked.

"It's the cobwebs," said the silvery grey person. "I don't know what to do about them."

The little old woman ran back into the house and picked up her broom and a basket of dusters.

"Just tell me where they are," she said fiercely. "I've never met a cobweb yet that didn't whisk away when I got busy."

The silvery grey person waved his arms in the air, and silver dust scattered about him.

"Up there," he whispered, "seventeen times as high as the moon."

The little old woman looked up into the night sky. Sure enough, there, high above the moon, were long trails of cobweb lying across the sky. She hurried inside, and shook the little old man from his doze in front of the rosy crackling fire.

"Come along, my dear," she said, "I need your help."

Nibbler and Plum ran out with the little old man, but when Nibbler saw the stranger he began to whine. He lowered his head, and crawled back into the house with his tail tucked under him. Plum was not afraid. She greeted the grey person as an old friend, purring and rubbing in and out of his legs.

"Whatever is it?" asked the little old man.

"We need your help," said the little old woman. She shook the dusters out of the basket, and settled herself and her broom inside.

"Now my dear, toss me up, just as high as ever you can."

The little old man picked up the basket.

*Then, with a heave and a pitch and a toss, he threw
the little old woman up and up and up into the air.*

He shut his eyes and counted to three. Then, with a heave and a pitch and a toss, he threw the little old woman up and up and up into the air. Up she flew, higher and higher, until the little old man could only see her as a tiny speck against the light of the moon.

The silvery grey stranger bowed a long and quivery bow.

"I do thank you," he said in his soft thread of a voice, and he shook himself all over. Silvery sparkles flew in the air and settled on the little old man and on the ground around him; it made him sneeze – once, twice, three times.

When he had stopped sneezing the stranger was gone – flown back to his home in the moon. Looking up, the old man could see his pale face smiling down.

★ ★ ★

The little old woman came back with the sunlight in the early morning. She slept a little in her rocking chair, and then bustled about the house. It seemed to the little old man that she was not as quick as usual. Perhaps she was tired?

When evening came the little old man put on the kettle, and sat down in front of the fire. Nibbler and Plum sat down with him, and so did the little old woman.

"That's a fine night's work," said the little old man, looking up into the clear and starlit sky. "Not a trace of a cobweb can I see."

The little old woman sniffed. "Indeed, I should hope not, my dear," she said. "When has a cobweb ever been too much for me and my broom? I shall be up again next full moon, just to make sure."

"Would you like a little cup of cocoa?"

"That's a fine night's work," said the little old man,
looking up into the clear and starlit sky.

the little old man asked.

"Indeed I would, my dear," said the little old woman. "And, if it's all the same to you, I'll just sit quietly here this evening. It's tiring work, sweeping all those cobwebs away."

The little old man and the little old woman sat happily together. Nibbler slept curled up at their feet, and Plum settled himself on the little old woman's lap.

It was the same the next night and every night until the full moon rose, and then once more the little old woman seated herself in her basket and the little old man tossed her up into the sky.

"Wheeeee!" she called, as she flew up and up and up. "Can you see me, my dear?"

"I can see you," the little old man said, smiling.

"Will you come with me next time the moon is full?" asked the little old woman.

"No, not I," said the little old man, and he went into the house as the little old woman flew up and away out of sight.

I'll sit by myself tonight, he thought as he put wood on the fire and the kettle on to boil, but she'll be here tomorrow and every night before the next full moon.

Up in the sky the little old woman was sweeping away the cobwebs. Down below the little old man was rocking in his chair, while the kettle bubbled happily on the hearth. The man in the moon smiled at them both, and the silver moon sparkles glistened and shone in the little old man's hair. Nibbler and Plum slept peacefully, and there was not so much as the smallest of sighs in the little old house under the moon.

In the middle of the world there was a forest of tall pine trees, and in among the pine trees was a wooden house.

LITTLE IVAN

In the middle of the world there was a forest of tall pine trees, and in among the pine trees was a wooden house. Little Ivan and his grandmother lived in the house, and very happy they were. Every day Grandmother went to work in the village beyond the forest, and before she went she would cook Little Ivan his dinner and leave it in the oven to keep warm.

"Now, Little Ivan, when are you to eat your dinner?"

"At twelve o'clock, Grandmother, and not before."

"You remember that, Little Ivan."

"I will, Grandmother, I will."

25

And Grandmother would set off on her long walk through the trees to the village. In the evening when she came home she and Little Ivan would eat their supper, and then if it was light they would walk under the trees and collect fir-cones. If it was dark they would sit in front of the fire and tell each other stories.

One morning Grandmother cooked Little Ivan a bowl of bacon and red beans, and put it in the oven to keep warm.

"Now, Little Ivan, when are you to eat your dinner?"

"At twelve o'clock, Grandmother, and not before."

"You remember that, Little Ivan."

"I will, Grandmother, I will."

And Grandmother put on her shawl and set off on her long walk through the trees. She hadn't gone very far when she heard singing – a wild singing that she hadn't heard in the woods for a long long time. Grandmother stopped and listened.

"Yoi! Yoi! Yoi!"

"*Well!*" said Grandmother to herself. "If I'm not much mistaken, that there is Old Mother Wolf, and if Old Mother Wolf is singing that song she's got wolf-cubs with her. And if she and her cubs have come to live in our forest then that means *trouble*. I'd better hurry home and tell Little Ivan." And Grandmother turned around and went hurrying back along the path to the wooden house.

Little Ivan was very surprised to see Grandmother coming back. "Whatever is it?" he asked.

Grandmother was wheezing and panting.

"Little Ivan," she puffed, "if I'm not much mistaken Old Mother Wolf has come

His bowl of bacon and red beans was in the oven, and the smell came out of the oven and into the kitchen.

to live in our forest. And if Old Mother Wolf is here with her wolf-cubs then that means *trouble*, so you be sure and keep the door and the windows *tight shut!*"

"Yes, Grandmother," said Little Ivan.

"You remember that, Little Ivan."

"I will, Grandmother, I will."

And Grandmother turned herself around again and went hurrying back along the path.

Little Ivan went back to playing with his fir-cones. His bowl of bacon and red beans was in the oven, and the smell came out of the oven and into the kitchen where Little Ivan was playing.

"Mmmmm ... that smells very good," thought Little Ivan.

The smell came out of the kitchen and into the house, and out of the house and into the forest. It floated away in and out of

29

the tall pine trees until it reached the very darkest part of the forest, and there it drifted down into a deep dark cave. Inside the cave was Mother Wolf and her three little wolf-cubs, and they all sat up and sniffed.

"Yip yip yip!" snapped the three little wolf-cubs. "That smells *very* good!"

"Yoi yoi yoi," said Mother Wolf. "It smells very good indeed. Shall I fetch it for you for your dinner?"

"Yes ess ess!" The three little wolf-cubs rubbed their tummies and rolled over and over.

"I'll be off then," said Mother Wolf, and she began running through the woods on her sneaky soft pitter-patter feet.

In and out of the tall trees she ran, until she came to Little Ivan's house, and when she reached the door she knocked three times.

Inside the cave was Mother Wolf and her three little wolf-cubs, and they all sat up and sniffed.

"Who's that?" said Little Ivan, and he ran to the window.

Mother Wolf leaped in the air and ran right around the house. She ran so fast that her ears blew back, and her whiskers whistled in the wind, and as she ran she called out,

*"Open the door just a crack, just a crack,
And I'll give you a ride on my back."*

I'd *love* to go as fast as that, thought Little Ivan, and he opened the door just as wide as a crack.

CRASH! Before Little Ivan had time to say hello or goodbye, Mother Wolf was in the house and running up and down the stairs. Into the kitchen she rushed, and she snatched the bowl of bacon and red beans from the oven. Then with a leap and a

He opened the door just as wide as a crack.

bound she was out of the door, and Little Ivan could only see the trees waving where she had dashed past. On and on through the trees she ran, until she saw the three little wolf-cubs sitting up and waiting for her.

"Here, my dears," she said. "Eat up and be glad."

And the three little wolf-cubs ate up all the bacon and red beans, and they licked their lips and they rubbed their tummies.

"Yummyummyumm," they said.

When Grandmother came home that evening Little Ivan was waiting at the door.

"Well, Little Ivan, did you enjoy your dinner today?"

Little Ivan shook his head.

"Why ever not?" Grandmother stared at him. "You're not going to tell me that you let Old Mother Wolf into the house?"

34

Little Ivan nodded miserably.

"*Well!* Don't you go expecting me to be sorry for you! Now tomorrow, you be sure and keep that door tightly *shut!*"

Little Ivan nodded again. "Oh, *yes*, Grandmother."

"T'ch t'ch t'ch," said Grandmother crossly, and she began to make their supper.

The next morning Grandmother cooked Little Ivan chicken and barley for his dinner, and she put the bowl in the oven to keep warm.

"Now, Little Ivan, when are you to eat your dinner?"

"At twelve o'clock, Grandmother, and not before."

"And what will you do with the door, Little Ivan?"

"Keep it tight shut, Grandmother."

"You remember that, Little Ivan."

"I will, Grandmother, I will."

And Grandmother put on her shawl and set off on her long walk through the trees. Little Ivan sat down to play with his fir-cones. The smell of the chicken and barley was already creeping out of the oven and into the kitchen, and Little Ivan nodded.

"That will taste very good at twelve o'clock."

The smell came out of the kitchen and into the house, and out of the house and into the forest. It floated away in and out of the tall pine trees until it reached the very darkest part of the forest, and there it drifted down into Mother Wolf's cave. The three little wolf-cubs jumped in the air.

"Yip yip yip! That smells even better than yesterday!"

"Yoi yoi yoi," said Mother Wolf. "It does

indeed. Shall I fetch it for you for your dinner?"

"Yes ess ess!" The three little wolf-cubs rubbed their tummies and skipped up and down.

"I'll be off then," said Mother Wolf, and she began running through the woods on her sneaky soft pitter-patter feet.

In and out of the tall trees she ran, until she came to Little Ivan's house, and when she reached the door she knocked three times.

"Who's that?" said Little Ivan, and he ran to the window to look out.

Mother Wolf leapt in the air and ran right around the house and right around again. She ran so fast that her ears blew back, and her whiskers whistled in the wind, and as she ran she called out,

"Open the window a crack, just a crack,
And I'll give you a ride on my back."

"I'd *love* to go as fast as that," thought Little Ivan, and he opened the window just as wide as a crack.

CRASH! Before Little Ivan had time to say please or thank you, Mother Wolf was in the house and running up and down the stairs. Into the kitchen she rushed, and snatched the bowl of chicken and barley from the oven. Then with a leap and a bound she was out of the door, and Little Ivan could only see the trees waving where she had dashed past. On and on through the trees she went, until she saw the three little wolf-cubs sitting up and waiting for her.

"Here my dears," she said. "Eat up and be glad."

And the three little wolf-cubs ate up all

*Into the kitchen she rushed, and snatched the bowl
of chicken and barley from the oven.*

the chicken and barley, and they licked their lips and rubbed their tummies.

"Yummyummyumm," they said.

When Grandmother came home that evening Little Ivan was standing by the window.

"Well, Little Ivan, did you enjoy your dinner today?"

Little Ivan shook his head.

"Oh, Little Ivan! You *didn't* let Old Mother Wolf into the house again?"

Little Ivan nodded miserably.

"*Well!*" Grandmother sat down on a chair with a flump. "Don't you go expecting me to be sorry for you! And don't go expecting any dinner tomorrow, either. I don't cook nice dinners for you to give to that old wolf and her family. You'll have bread and water tomorrow, and be thankful."

"Yes, Grandmother," said Little Ivan.

The next morning Grandmother got up later than usual. She cut Little Ivan a thick slice of bread and poured him out a glass of water, and then she locked the rest of the bread in the cupboard.

"There's your dinner, Little Ivan," she said. "And when are you to eat it?"

"At twelve o'clock, Grandmother."

"You remember that, Little Ivan, and mind that you eat it yourself."

"I will, Grandmother. I will."

And Grandmother put on her shawl and set off on her long walk though the trees. Little Ivan went slowly down to the kitchen, and looked sadly at the empty oven.

"No good dinner today," he thought, and picked up his fir-cones.

Mother Wolf and her three little wolf-cubs were sitting outside their cave sniffing the air.

"Where's our dinner, Mother?" asked the cubs.

Mother Wolf shook her head. "No dinner today, my dears."

"Ow ow ow!" howled the little wolf-cubs. "No dinner today!"

Mother Wolf sniffed the air again. "Perhaps Little Ivan has a cold dinner today? Cheese? A ham? A sausage?"

"Yip yip yip!" snapped the three little wolf-cubs. "Go and see, dear Mother, go and see."

"I'll be off, then," said Mother Wolf, and she began running through the woods on her sneaky soft pitter-patter feet.

In and out of the tall trees she ran, until she came to Little Ivan's house, and when she reached the door she knocked three times.

"That's Mother Wolf!" said Little Ivan,

and he ran into the kitchen. Quickly, quickly he ate his bread, and quickly, quickly he drank his water.

"There! Now I've eaten my dinner!" he said, and he hurried to the window.

Mother Wolf leapt in the air and ran right around the house three times. She ran so fast that her ears blew back and her whiskers whistled in the wind, and as she ran she called out,

"Open the door or the window a crack,
And I'll give you a ride on my back."

"Oh, how I'd *love* to go as fast as that," thought Little Ivan, and he flung open the window as wide as it would go.

WHOOSH! Mother Wolf leapt into the house, and ran up and down the stairs. Into the kitchen she rushed, but there she

He was so happy that he laughed and sang, and the wind carried his song far away beyond the trees.

stopped. There was nothing in the oven, and nothing on the shelf.

"I've eaten my dinner!" Little Ivan shouted, "now give me my ride!"

Mother Wolf stood very still. "Climb on to my back, Little Ivan," she said, "and hold on!"

Little Ivan climbed on to Mother Wolf's back, and with a leap and a bound she was out of the window. Little Ivan held on tightly to her rough tough fur. They were going so fast that the trees were a green blur on either side of them, and Little Ivan's hair streamed behind him. He was so happy that he laughed and sang, and the wind carried his song far away beyond the trees.

"*Oh!*" Little Ivan gasped as Mother Wolf carried him right into the middle of her dark, cold cave.

"*Ow!*" said Little Ivan as the three little

wolf-cubs pulled his hair and bit his fingers and scratched his feet.

"No dinner today, my dears," said Mother Wolf, "but I've brought you something to play with. It's too thin to eat, but we'll keep it to sweep and to dust and to clean. Won't that be nice?"

"Yes ess ess!" said the cubs, and they rolled Little Ivan over and over until he was dusty and dirty and very unhappy indeed.

Grandmother saw the wide open window when she was still a long way away. "Oh dear, oh dear, oh *dear*!" she said, and hurried up the path. "Little Ivan! Where are you?"

There was no answer. Grandmother called again, but all that she could hear was the wind hushing the trees.

"I do believe that Old Mother Wolf has taken my Little Ivan away," Grandmother

They rolled Little Ivan over and over until he was dusty and dirty and very unhappy indeed.

said at last. "Oh dearie, dearie me – whatever shall I do?" And she began puffing and panting back the way she had come.

When she reached the village, she saw the children's band marching round and round the village square. "Tantantara! Boom boom boom! Squeak eek tiddle squeak eek!" When the children saw Grandmother hurrying down the path towards them they stopped at once and ran to meet her.

"What is it, Grandmother? Don't cry, we'll help you!" Grandmother wiped her eyes.

"It's Old Mother Wolf," she said. "I think she's taken my Little Ivan, and I don't know what to do."

"We'll fetch him back," said one of the children. "We'll blow our trumpets!"

"And bang our drums!"

"And play our violins!"

"We'll play Old Mother Wolf the loudest tune she's ever heard!"

Grandmother blew her nose, and began to smile. "You've given me such an idea. I know *just* what to do now. Shall we be off?"

"Yes yes yes!" shouted all the children.

"Shhhh!" said Grandmother. "We must be very quiet."

"Shhhh!" said all the children, and they began to tiptoe in and out of the tall pine trees under the light of the moon.

The forest was very dark all around Mother Wolf's home. The children followed Grandmother until they all stood in a line outside the deep dark cave, and they watched and they listened.

"Zzzzzz zzzzzzz zzzzzzz."

"I think Old Mother Wolf is asleep," whispered Grandmother. "Are the trumpeters ready?"

"Yes, Grandmother," whispered the children.

"One, two, three – PLAY!"

"Tantara! Tantara! Tantara!" went the trumpets.

Down at the bottom of the cave Mother Wolf and the wolf-cubs and Little Ivan woke up with a start.

"What a horrible noise!" said Mother Wolf crossly. Little wolf-cub, tell them to go away!"

The first little wolf-cub ran up to the top of the cave. "Please go away," he said. But before he could say anything more, Grandmother snatched him up and wrapped him tightly in her shawl.

"That's one," she whispered. "Are the drummers ready?"

"Ready, Grandmother," whispered the children.

*But before he could say anything more,
Grandmother snatched him up.*

"One, two, three – PLAY!"

"Boom! Boom! Boom!" went the drums.

Down at the bottom of the cave Mother Wolf shook her head.

"That's even louder than last time," she said. "Little wolf-cub, tell them to go away."

The second little wolf-cub ran up to the top of the cave. "Go away," she said, but before she could say anything more, Grandmother snatched her up and wrapped her tightly in her shawl.

"That's two," whispered Grandmother. "Are the violins ready?"

"Ready, Grandmother," whispered the children.

"One, two, three – PLAY!"

"Squeak eek tiddle squeak eek!" went the violins.

Down at the bottom of the cave Mother Wolf was growing angry.

"That's a terrible noise," she said. "How can I sleep with a noise like that going on? Little wolf-cub, go and tell them that if they don't go away *at once* I will come and eat them all up."

The third little wolf-cub ran up to the top of the cave, and looked around at Grandmother and all the children.

"If you don't go away *at once*," he said, "Mother Wolf will eat you all up!"

"Oh, she will, will she?" said Grandmother, and she snatched up the little wolf-cub and wrapped him up in her shawl with his brother and sister.

"That's three!" said Grandmother. "Now, is everybody ready?"

"Ready!" said the children.

"One, two, three – PLAY!" said Grandmother. And all the children began to play together.

"Tantara! Boom! Squeak eek tiddle!"

Down at the bottom of the cave Mother Wolf was very angry indeed.

"This is *too much*!" she said, and she rushed up to the top of the cave with her sharp white teeth shining in the moonlight.

"If you don't go away," she snarled, "I shall eat you all up from the tops of your heads to the tips of your toes!"

"Just one minute, Mother Wolf," said Grandmother. "Let me tell you that I've caught your three little wolf-cubs, and I'm not giving them back until I have my Little Ivan safe and sound."

"Mother! Mother! Mother!" called the three little wolf-cubs bundled up in Grandmother's shawl.

Mother Wolf sat down in front of her cave and scratched her ear.

"Very well," she said. "He's too thin for a

dinner." And she turned round and went down into the cave.

A moment later Little Ivan came crawling out. He was dusty and dirty and scratched and bitten, but when he saw Grandmother he shouted, "GRANDMOTHER!"

"LITTLE IVAN!" shouted Grandmother, and they hugged each other as hard as they could while all the children cheered.

"Now," Grandmother said, "let's see about these little wolf-cubs." She unwrapped them all from her shawl, and they ran to Mother Wolf.

"We want our dinners!" they cried, "we're hungry!"

"Shall we go over the hills and far away?" said Mother Wolf.

"Yes ess ess!" said the three little wolf-cubs, and they and Mother Wolf ran away, in and out of the tall trees and out of the

*And they held Little Ivan's hands and ran with him
through the trees to the wooden house.*

forest and over the hills on their sneaky soft pitter-patter feet while above them the moon shone down.

"Well!" said Grandmother. "That's well gone! And now let's all go home."

"Hurrah!" shouted all the children. And they held Little Ivan's hands and ran with him through the trees to the wooden house.

Grandmother made them all a fine feast, and when they had eaten as much as they could, they sat down and told stories of woods and wolves and forests and fir-cones. And the next morning when Grandmother went down the path to work she took Little Ivan with her, and he went to school with all the other children, so if ever Old Mother Wolf came to sing her songs again in the forest of tall pine trees in the middle of the world there would be nobody there to hear her.

A little fire flickered in the grate, but there was no more wood left in the broken basket by the chimney.

THE APPLE CHILD

There was once a cold village on the side of a tall cold mountain. Behind the village was a stony field where a flock of thin sheep huddled together under the shadow of a few spindly apple trees, and high above the mountain hung the moon; a pale cold moon that sent long dark shadows sprawling along the ground, creeping in and out of the village, and crouching down beside Ben's small cold cottage.

"*Brrrr*," shivered Ben, pulling an old sack round his shoulders. A little fire flickered in the grate, but there was no more wood left in the broken basket by the chimney. He got up and stared out of the window. Up on the mountainside he could see the apple trees quivering in the wind.

"I'll run up and see if there are any twigs or sticks under the trees," said Ben. He wrapped the sack more closely about himself, and slipped out of the cottage and up the street. The wind caught him and tugged and pulled at him, but he put his head down and trudged on to where the cold field lay beyond the last house.

The sheep shifted unwillingly as Ben walked among them; "Saaaad," they bleated, "saaad!" The trees were moaning and muttering to each other, the wind snapped at their branches and whipped their last few leaves off and away.

High in the sky the moon gazed down. Ben glanced up, and for a moment thought he saw a watching silver face.

"What can I do, Moon?" he called. "I'm

cold – I'm ever so cold!"

There was no answer from the moon, but the wind suddenly dropped. Just for a moment there was a stillness, a silence as if all the moonlit world was holding its breath. Only a moment it lasted, and then up sprang the wind with a howl and a shriek, and tore the sack from his back. The trees bent and swayed, and with a loud crash a long branch fell to the ground beside him.

"Thank you! Thank you!" Ben shouted, and he picked up the branch and ran as fast as he could back to his small cold cottage. The fire was a mere glimmer, but as he fed it first the smallest twig and then the bigger ones, it began to take heart and to glow warmly. Breaking the branch, he built the fire up higher, until the shadows were dancing and the smell of apple wood filled the room.

"*Oh!*" Ben stared as the flames sparkled

and crackled and burnt red and green and silver.

CRACK! A log of the apple wood split into two halves, and a small green child no bigger than Ben's hand stepped out of the fire and on to the floor beside him.

"Good evening," said the child.

Ben couldn't speak. He stared and stared at the little green figure, and looked into the fire, and then back again.

"If you're wondering where I come from," said the child, "I come from the apple log. I'm an apple child – how do you do, and what's your name?"

"I'm Ben," said Ben, still staring.

The apple child smiled. "Glad to meet you. And now, how about supper?"

Ben shook his head. "I'm sorry," he said, "I've nothing but a few old seed potatoes in a sack in the yard."

*A small green child no bigger than Ben's hand
stepped out of the fire.*

"Let's fetch them in," said the apple child. "There's nothing like a big baked potato."

Ben shook his head again. How could an apple child know that seed potatoes were poor shrivelled green things that could never be eaten? He went slowly out into the bitterly cold wind.

The sack was behind the door, just where the farmer had left it. The sack was there – but it wasn't nearly empty. To Ben's amazement, it was full to splitting with fine, clean, rich yellow potatoes. He chose four of the biggest and hurried back inside.

"Put them to bake on the fire," said the apple child. "I'm hungry!"

Ben slept well that night. He woke in the morning to find the sun bursting in through the window.

"Good morning," said a cheerful voice. "Shall we have eggs for our breakfast?"

Ben rubbed his eyes, and saw the apple child standing beside him holding two big brown eggs.

"That's a splendid black hen you have," said the apple child. "She's hiding a nest behind the blackberry bushes."

"But she's been gone for months," Ben said. "I was certain the fox had had her for dinner."

"Not she," said the apple child. "And I found a few good nuts on the walnut tree."

Ben looked curiously at the apple child. Had he grown in the night? It seemed to Ben that he had, although he was still the smallest child he had ever seen. And what magic was he working? Even Ben's bare cold room felt full of warmth and the smell of apple wood and sunshine and flowers.

*When Mrs Wutherlop came by to ask if he could
spare an egg or two he was more than willing.*

"Well?" asked the apple child. "Have you decided? Soft or hard-boiled eggs?"

Ben and the apple child settled down happily. It seemed to Ben that the cottage was always warm now, and full of sunlight. The black hen was laying steadily, and his two little brown and white bantams had reappeared, clucking happily, from under the hawthorn hedge. Ben was quite sure that he had, with his very own eyes, seen them both being carried off by foxes, but he smiled and collected the small brown eggs. When Mrs Wutherlop from next door came by to ask if he could spare an egg or two he was more than willing, and he took the crusty bread she offered him in exchange with pleasure.

Strong green shoots sprang up in Ben's bare back garden, and he found that he was growing the finest cabbages and leeks and carrots in the village – more than enough for him and the apple child. Ben filled his wheelbarrow and took his extra vegetables to the shop, and came home chinking real money in his pocket, the first he had had for weeks and months and years. He didn't see old Mrs Crabbitty in the opposite cottage peering out of her misted and cobwebbed windows as he hopped along the road, and he didn't see Mrs Crabbitty poking and sniffing at the crisp green cabbages and creamy white leeks in the shop, her little black eyes gleaming greedily.

"Them's Ben's leeks, you says? And carrotses? Well, well, well…" and she shuffled home, mumbling to herself.

That evening Mrs Crabbitty came knocking on Ben's door.

"Seems things is a-picking up for you,

young man," she said, her eyes slipping and sliding as she stared over Ben's shoulder into the glowing room beyond. "Seems as if you found yourself a liddle slip of luck."

Ben felt uncomfortable. He had never liked Mrs Crabbitty, with her peeking nose and her small black shiny eyes, but he knew she lived on what she could beg or borrow from the village, and had nothing of her own.

"Would you care to come in?" he asked, with a small sigh.

"There now," said Mrs Crabbitty, whisking through the door and settling herself by the crackling flames. "There's a fine fire."

Ben looked around. He had last seen the apple child toasting his toes on the hearth, but there was no sign of him now. He felt Mrs Crabbitty's beady black eyes searching round and about, and he hastily turned back to her.

"Looking for something?" Mrs Crabbitty asked him. "Or, maybe, for someone?"

Ben shook his head.

Mrs Crabbitty brought two shining steel knitting needles out of her pocket, and a small ball of grey, greasy wool. She began to knit, and while she knitted she swayed a little and hummed a strange tuneless drone.

Ben couldn't take his eyes away from the flashing silver needles, and when Mrs Crabbitty began to ask him questions about the garden, and the little black hen, and the never-ending supply of wood in the basket, he was unable to stop himself telling her all about his visit to the moonlit orchard, and the coming of the apple child.

"So, you just threw the wood on the fire,

*She began to knit, and while she knitted she swayed
a little, and hummed a strange tuneless drone.*

young man?" Mrs Crabbitty asked, clicking her needles and swaying.

"Yes," Ben said, his voice creeping away from him like a small sly snake.

"Then what's good for the young will be good for us old ones," said Mrs Crabbitty. She sat up straight, and snapped the shining needles together. Hauling herself up on to her feet she nodded at Ben.

"I'll be off to my own poor place," she said. "But I'll be having a special sort of a blaze tonight, nows I knows what's what."

Ben watched her scuttle away. He was surprised to see that she didn't go straight home, but went away down the road, pulling her shawl round her shoulders.

Mrs Crabbitty scurried along towards the end of the village street.

"I'll fetch meself a slice of luck," she said,

rubbing her hands together. A sharp gust of wind caught at her shawl and tossed it away in front of her until it caught on the branch of a tall tree standing at the very edge of the orchard.

"Dratted wind!" Mrs Crabbitty struggled towards the tree, and pulled at her shawl. It came with a wrench, and brought a shower of twigs and a twisted branch with it that fell at her feet.

"Well, well, well." Mrs Crabbitty bent and picked up the branch. "Maybe here's me luck, after all." And she hurried back towards her dark and dusty house. The wind grew louder than ever, and rushed in between the apple trees with a shriek so that they shook and quivered under the moon.

Mrs Crabbitty's fire was a mere glimmer in the darkness of her dusty, spidered room, but she fed it with pieces of loose bark until

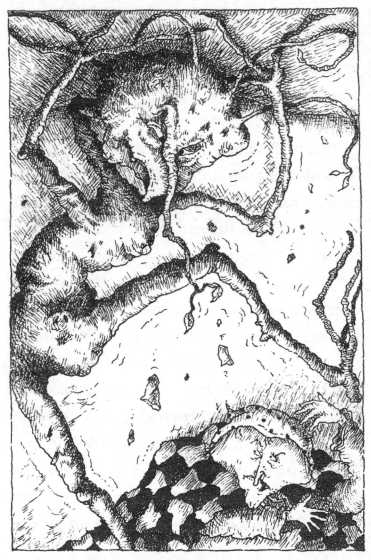

Mrs Crabbitty saw it bulge and stretch and twist until it was pressed up against her ceiling.

an uncertain flame flickered. Then she took the entire branch, and pushed it into the back of the fireplace. First one green flame and then another sprang up, but there was no heat to be felt; the blaze was as cold as the fire at the heart of a bitter green emerald.

"Now, I'd like company, so's all me work gets done for me. No reason why lazy boys should have all the luck."

Mrs Crabbitty peered into the grate, and the branch began to twist. There was a splitting and a splintering, and something shapeless came slithering out on to the hearth. It squirmed itself into a long-bodied, bandy-legged, large-headed creature, and then it began to grow. Mrs Crabbitty, watching open mouthed, saw it bulge and stretch and twist until it was pressed up against her cracked and yellowed ceiling. Only then did it stop growing. Mrs Crabbitty reached behind her for her chair, and sat down with a flump. The creature turned and looked at her with its glassy eyes, and she stared back.

"What kind of a thing ezactly are you?"

"Elder Bogle," growled the creature in a voice that was full of gravel and grit.

"Ah," said Mrs Crabbitty. "And why ain't you an apple child to help a poor woman?"

"Elder branch." The bogle pointed a bent and wrinkled finger at the smouldering fire.

"Is that so? And what ezactly can you do?"

A movement on the table caught Mrs Crabbitty's eye, and turning she saw a bowl of small apples blackening and rotting as she watched. The elder bogle watched as well, and as the last apple shrank into nothingness he smiled a sour and twisted smile.

Mrs Crabbitty sucked her lower lip thoughtfully.

"If you and I is to live together," she said, "I'll thank you to leave *my* goodies alone."

The elder bogle gave her a cold look, but it said nothing. It folded itself up into a dark heap, and appeared to go to sleep. Mrs Crabbitty took her shawl and climbed up to bed. Before she went to sleep she thought for a long time and then, smiling, closed her eyes.

Ben and the apple child heard about the elder bogle from Mrs Wutherlop. She came knocking on the cottage door the next morning, carrying a jug of sour milk and a dish of moulded and pitted plums.

"What is it?" Ben asked. "What's happened?"

Mrs Wutherlop began to cry. "Mrs Crabbitty," she sobbed, "her said that if I don't give her milk each day she'd witch me. And I says no, an' she whistles up a horrible bogle thing, an' now there's nothing fit to eat in my larder, nor yet a green leaf in my garden, an' the kitten's crying its heart out. And it's the same to all the folks in the village who won't do what she says, up comes that there bogle, an' the milk turns sour an' the hens don't lay an' the pigsies are as thin as a rail. And us doesn't know what to!" Mrs Wutherlop sat down on Ben's step and threw her apron over her head.

Ben patted Mrs Wutherlop's shoulder, but she went on crying. He hurried out to his own garden, but there everything was growing and green. He peeped over the fence, and at once saw the terrible bareness where Mrs Wutherlop's carrots and onions and potatoes had been. Even the holly tree was as bare as a winter's oak.

Mrs Wutherlop sat down on Ben's step
and threw her apron over her head.

Ben picked up a basket and filled it with walnuts and eggs and apples and cabbages from his larder, and put it down beside the still sobbing Mrs Wutherlop. Then he went to see if the apple child knew what might be happening.

The apple child was, as usual, sitting and feeding the fire with twigs and sticks.

"There's something terrible come to the village!" Ben said. The apple child nodded. "Mrs Crabbitty's slice of luck."

Ben squatted down by the child. "Is there anything we can do?" he asked. "Poor Mrs Wutherlop's crying and crying and crying. Can you make her garden grow again like you made mine?"

The apple child stood up and stretched. "There's not room for an elder bogle and an apple child in the one village," he said.

"What do you mean?" Ben asked

anxiously. "You don't mean you're going to go away?"

The apple child smiled. "We'll see," he said. "Elder Bogles are strong, but they're not always clever."

"I'll come with you," said Ben, as the apple child moved towards the door. "I'm not scared – well, not very."

Ben and the apple child walked out of the cottage and past Mrs Wutherlop. She had stopped crying, and was holding the basket of vegetables closely to herself as if they were protection. When she saw Ben and the apple child going across to Mrs Crabbitty's cottage she followed them.

Mrs Crabbitty was sitting on a bench at the side of her cracked and crumbling cottage. She was shelling a bowl of fresh peas, and six or seven fine fat hens were

*The apple child was looking up at the little windows
of the cottage where a dark shadow was moving.*

clucking and fussing about her feet. Piled up against her cottage wall were strings of onions, jugs of thick golden cream, sweet cured hams, pies and pastries with shining sugar crusts, russet apples and a huge grass twist of strawberries. There was no sign of the elder bogle.

Mrs Crabbitty looked up and saw Ben and the apple child. Her face looked pinched and sour and as if she too was growing moulded and rotten.

"And what would you be after?" Her voice sounded thinner and sharper. "These things is all mine, mind you. Mrs Crabbitty's found her luck."

Ben didn't know what to say. The apple child was saying nothing at all. He was looking up at the little windows of the cottage where a dark shadow was moving behind the dust and the cobwebs. There was a slithering and a sliding, and the doorway was filled with the twisted shape of the elder bogle. When it saw the apple child it began to hiss, and its eyes glowed greedily.

"Now, my pet," said Mrs Crabbitty, "what's troubling you?"

The elder bogle cracked its bony knuckles and stretched out its skinny arm towards the apple child.

"Go away," it growled. It waved at the house behind it, and the village in front. "MINE! ALL MINE!"

The apple child still said nothing, but he shook his head. The elder bogle began to snarl.

"Fight!" Its teeth were long and yellow, and Ben took a step backwards. He was glad to find Mrs Wutherlop close behind him, and she put a large freckled hand on his shoulder.

"FIGHT!" The elder bogle was circling round the apple child, growling and sniffing and snarling.

"Wait." The child's voice was small but very clear. "I won't fight, but I challenge you: a test – a test of strength."

The elder bogle and Mrs Crabbitty both laughed a sour, cackling laugh, and then the elder bogle nodded its heavy head. It turned round and round until it saw the tall old pine tree that sheltered Mrs Crabbitty's cottage. Crouching down, it clasped its long arms about the tree's huge trunk, and then with a grunt and a heave it wrenched the quivering tree out of the ground. With a gravelly snarl it stood up, the pine on its shoulder, and began to make its way up the mountain towards a wind-blasted tree at the very top.

Mrs Crabbitty gave a shrill scream of laughter. "There, my fine friends. He can carry the tallest tree on his shoulder, all the way up to the top and all the way down. A test of strength, you says – I says the same – can you do as well? Look, see, already he's at the top!"

Ben watched in horror. Even with the massive pine tree on his back the elder bogle was leaping and jumping across the rough mountainside. The apple child was as light as the wind, how could he possibly carry any such load?

The apple child seemed unconcerned. He was choosing an apple from Mrs Wutherlop's basket, and when he had carefully chosen one he polished it on his sleeve.

"Huzzah! Huzzah! Here comes my pet,

*The elder bogle was leaping and jumping
across the rough mountainside.*

my pretty poppet!" Mrs Crabbitty waved her bony arms in the air as the elder bogle came loping back down the village street. It was still carrying the pine tree on one shoulder, and on the other shoulder was a massive branch from the stricken tree on the top of the mountain. With a snarl of victory it slid to a stop in front of Mrs Crabbitty, and tossed the huge pine tree right over her cottage. Ben felt the ground shudder under his feet, and a trembling in the air as the old pine crashed to the earth.

"YOU!" shouted the elder bogle, sneering down at the apple child.

The apple child nodded. He touched Ben with his hand, and sprang away up the street towards the mountain. He ran as if he was dancing, and the apple trees fluttered and rustled as he passed them. He ran as if he was flying, and the birds overhead swooped lower and circled above his head. He spun three times round the tree at the very top of the mountain, and then ran back to the village with the ease of a stream flowing over a grassy bank. He touched Ben once again, and the time that he had taken was less than half that taken by the elder bogle.

"I say the apple child wins!" called out Ben, but his voice was uncertain. The elder bogle and Mrs Crabbitty snorted, and the elder bogle stamped its leathery foot so hard that a grey dust flew up, making Ben cough and rub his eyes.

"You called for a test of strength," said Mrs Crabbitty, shaking her fist. "And I says as my pretty pet is the winner!"

The elder bogle grinned a wicked yellow-toothed grin, and rubbed its gnarled and withered hands together. Mrs Crabbitty

In his hand was an apple, and as
they all stared at him he broke it in half.

pointed at Ben. "You and yours have had your chances. So, be off with you!"

Ben's shoulders drooped, and he nodded hopelessly.

"We'll go," he said, and turned away.

"Just one moment."

The apple child was standing in front of them. In his hand was an apple, and as they all stared at him he broke it in half, and showed it to the elder bogle.

"Six pips," he said. "Six seeds – SO! You carried *one* tree, but I carried *six* apple trees up and round the mountain ... six tiny living trees in one apple. I am the winner, and I claim the village for my own."

The elder bogle let out a shriek that made Ben clutch his ears. Mrs Crabbitty screamed, a high piercing scream.

"Tricksied! We've been tricksied!"

The elder bogle howled and wailed and

stamped his foot. The earth beneath Ben's feet shook, and a swirl of grey-green dust flew up into the air. The elder bogle stamped again, and the ground split beneath him.

"No! My poppitty! My pet!" Mrs Crabbitty sank on to her knees, but the elder bogle was already gone. All that was left was a clump of green leaves.

"Oh! Oh! Oh!" said Mrs Crabbitty, and she turned and scuttled into her cottage like a small frightened spider.

The apple child looked after her. "She'll do no harm now," he said.

Mrs Wutherlop took Ben's arm.

"A nice cup of tea wouldn't come amiss. Eh, what a carry on!"

Ben turned to the apple child. "Is it all over? Should we go home?"

"Yes," said the apple child. "Hurry on home."

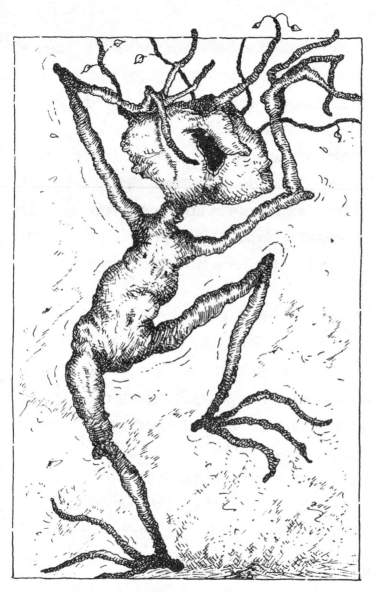

The elder bogle stamped again,
and the ground split beneath him.

Something in his voice made Ben stare at him. "Aren't you coming too?"

The apple child shook his head. "I'll be about," he said. "Here and there…"

Ben sighed. "I shall miss you," he said.

Mrs Wutherlop patted Ben's shoulder. "You can come and sit with me for company," she said. "And I've a kitten that's looking for a home."

The apple child waved, and moved towards the apple trees on the mountainside.

They were heavy with ripe red apples, and the sheep grazing beneath were fat and thickly fleeced. Even the bare mountainside was flushed with patches of soft green grass and clusters of bushes.

"Goodbye, Ben," said the apple child.

"Goodbye," said Ben, "and thank you." He could feel tears at the back of his eyes, and there was a lump in his throat. Turning, he ran after the warm and comfortable figure of Mrs Wutherlop. The apple child paused for a moment, and then slipped in among the apple trees.

On the edge of the deepening blue sky a golden harvest moon was rising, and high above a single star watched over the village. Shadows stretched out from the richly laden trees, like thick ribbons of warm black velvet binding the small houses and cottages safely together, and the moon smiled as it sailed on over the mountain.

THE

END